THE ORP

PLIGHT

VICTORIAN ROMANCE

Catharine Dobbs

Contents

Chapter One Desperate Treading 3

Chapter Two Worked to the Bone 11

Chapter Three A Moment of Kindness 19

Chapter Four Desperate Times...27

Chapter Five Death Never Becomes the End.......................35

Chapter Six A Chance Encounter 43

Chapter Seven A Glimpse of Happiness................................51

Chapter Eight Threat of Separation 59

Chapter Nine No Choice 67

Chapter Ten A New Start 75

Epilogue: 83

Chapter One
Desperate Treading

Adelle looked up as another bout of chesty coughing came from beside the dwindling fire. Her mother was huddled in several thin blankets, shivering as she tried to get as close as she could to the fire. The flames were beginning to go out, and Adelle could already feel the chill. Clearly, her mother was feeling it worse. She lowered her sewing. "Mother?"

Beth Mallory sniffled and looked up. Her face was pale, almost flaxen. Her eyes were watery. Adelle's heart broke as she looked at the woman who had done everything and more in her power to look after her and her younger brother. Beth had managed to find strength from somewhere to go out and work as well as looking after her children and the apartment. Her husband, Adelle's father, had been proud of her.

Now she looked like a shadow of her former self. It was frightening to witness.

"I'm fine, darling." Beth managed a weak smile. "It's nothing." Then she was coughing again.

Adelle winced at the noise. "That doesn't sound fine, Mother. It sounds like your cough is getting worse."

"It's nothing I can't handle." Beth snorted. She frowned at her daughter, gesturing at the dress Adelle had laid out on her lap. "You worry about your work. I thought you had to get that dress done for tomorrow. Mrs Lacey won't be impressed if it isn't completed."

Adelle flushed and ducked her head. She knew her mother was right. Adelle hadn't been able to complete the alterations in time, and Mrs Lacey had acquiesced, for the first time, that she could take it home to complete it. If she didn't get it done, she would be out of a job. Adelle desperately needed this money. Beth's job as a teacher didn't pay much, which was why Adelle had left school after her father's death to start working.

Thirteen and she was struggling to keep her family afloat. Adelle just wanted to scream. It was unfair. All she wanted to do was be a child. Enjoy her youth. But she had had to grow up too fast. Adelle wasn't sure if she was capable of keeping up.

"Adelle."

She looked up.

Beth was looking at her as if she was about to cry. Her mother let out a shuddering sigh and tugged the blankets tighter around her shoulders. "Forgive me, my darling. I didn't mean to be terse with you. You don't deserve it, not when you work so hard."

Adelle had to swallow back the hard lump in her throat. Her fingers were starting to freeze up, and it was getting difficult to get them to work. Her work wasn't even half-done, but it had to be completed. Even if it meant drawing blood whenever the needle pierced her skin.

She managed a smile at her mother. "Things aren't easy at the moment for any of us, Mother. We're all on edge, and you're unwell."

She couldn't bring herself to be angry at her mother. Her father had died the year before, influenza taking him very swiftly. After that, Beth seemed to have gone to pieces. She hadn't always been a strong woman with regard to her health, but now it had deteriorated. Adelle was frightened she would wake up and see her mother dead beside her.

Nothing could bring her to be angry knowing that the older woman's days might be numbered.

Beth was looking at her daughter in wonder. She shook her head. "How did I end up with a child who has grown up so wise?" she murmured.

"Father was a good teacher."

"That he was. You're so much like him." Beth sighed sadly. "I just wish Elbert had paid more attention to his teachings."

It was the way she said it that had Adelle wincing. Her younger brother was at the same school where their mother taught. And while Adelle had been a determined worker, Elbert was the complete opposite. Every day, Beth came home irritated with her son. Elbert just would not settle.

And it had gotten worse since their father passed away.

"Has he been in trouble again?" Adelle asked.

"I'm afraid so. He answered back to his mistress several times, and then he got his hands covered in ink after writing his lines."

Adelle raised her eyebrows. "You do realise that keeping our hands clean of ink when writing is never easy. We are only children."

"But not to the extent your brother did it." Beth shook her head with a frown. "The boy is just infuriating. He's a smart child when he wants to be. He just doesn't use the brain he was given."

Adelle silently agreed. She couldn't begin to imagine how embarrassing it was for her mother to know that her son was getting caned every other day, to hear his screams when the cane hit his hands. Elbert's fingers often turned black and blue, but he just kept going. It was as if he didn't care.

"I'm just glad you were good at school, Adelle." Beth started coughing again. "Or things would have been worse for me."

"A bit like that cough, Mother."

"I'll manage." Beth rubbed her chest, her breathing now sounding rattling. "Don't worry about me, Adelle."

"But I do worry, Mother," Adelle protested. "It's not even been a year since Father passed. I don't want you to go as well."

Beth's expression softened. She reached over and clasped her daughter's hand. Her fingers were even colder than Adelle's.

"I know, love." She smiled and squeezed Adelle's fingers. "And I'm not going anywhere."

If she had a bit more colour in her cheeks, Adelle might have believed it. But Beth looked close to death's door herself. Adelle bit her tongue and smiled back. She didn't want to think about that. Her mother was tougher than this; she would be fine.

That didn't sound as confident as it had been when Adelle was younger.

Beth settled back and curled in the direction of the fire. Soon she was asleep, snoring softly. Adelle carried on with her work, biting back winces as the needle kept pricking her fingers. This needed to be completed, or she would have no job tomorrow. Mrs Lacey had been lenient in some respects, mostly due to Adelle's youth, but she wouldn't be this time. This was an important piece of work, and the client wouldn't have it late on any circumstances.

Soon, Adelle had worked up enough warmth in her fingers to keep herself going. It wasn't long before she was flying through, completing the final stitch by the time the fire had gone out and the candle was about to extinguish. The darkness had crept in long ago, leaving Adelle to put aside her work in the moonlight coming through the curtain-less window. The moonlight cast a silvery sheen into the room.

Adelle glanced at the clock and saw the time. Elbert should have been back by now. He had been told to stay behind, due to his bad behaviour, to finish off his lines. This was the latest he had ever been home from school. If Beth was feeling better, she would have scolded Elbert for it.

Now Adelle would have to deal with her wayward little brother.

She jumped when there was a loud bang, a little boy's voice echoing through the sparse apartment, "Mother! I'm home!"

Adelle sighed and put aside her work. Beth was in no fit state to deal with her son, who thought he could act like the lord of the manor, swanning in whenever he thought he could. The boy was only ten; he had no authority over anybody. Elbert thought far too far above his station.

Her little brother was in the doorway, kicking off his boots. They had left a trail of mud across the hall. Adelle winced when she saw it. Something else she would have to clean up.

"Hello, Adelle." Elbert was still talking loudly. "Where's Mother?"

"She's sleeping, so you need to keep your voice down." Adelle frowned at her brother. "Where have you been, Elbert?"

"What?" Elbert's eyes widened. "I've just been out playing with my friends."

"You mean you've been getting into trouble again?" Adelle folded her arms. "Your friends are troublemakers. It's a wonder you haven't been arrested for your actions."

Elbert scowled. Like Adelle, he was raven-haired, and it was unruly. Even at such a young age, it was startling how alike he was to their late father. Right down to the scowl. "I don't answer to you, Adelle." Elbert snapped.

"Mother is ill and not able to deal with you as she should, so you do answer to me." Adelle rubbed at her head. She could feel a headache coming on. "Why do you keep getting into trouble, Elbert? You know it's embarrassing for us."

Elbert pouted, folding his arms with a scowl. "I don't like school," he said stoutly. "I want to play."

Adelle sighed. "We can't afford for you to do that. Father's gone and Mother's unwell. You and I need to make sure we can do whatever we can to help her." She gave her brother a very stern look. "You're just the right size to be shoved up a chimney, you know."

Elbert's face went pale. He hated confined spaces. It had him screaming like a stuck pig. Beth had given him a choice of becoming an apprentice chimney sweep or going to school, and Elbert had reluctantly chosen the latter. Adelle could tell he didn't want to contemplate the former.

"Mother won't let that happen to me." Elbert said defiantly. But he was still pale, chewing at his lower lip. "She's not going to die. Is she?"

Adelle glanced towards the living room. Beth hadn't stirred in spite of Elbert's loud entrance. She closed the door and knelt in front of her brother, cupping his grimy face in her hands. "If we don't get the money coming in, then she might. We can't afford a doctor for her. We can't even afford heating to keep her warm."

Elbert looked like he was about to cry. He sniffed loudly, wiping his nose on his sleeve. Then he drew himself up to his full height, squaring his shoulders. "I can go and ask a couple of friends if I can have some logs for the fire," he suggested. "They've allowed me to do it before."

They had done it previously, but Adelle knew they had to be careful. Everyone they knew was suffering as much as they were. Their neighbours helped out within reason, but there was only so much Adelle could ask for. Elbert was less inclined to think about that and more concerned about their mother. He wanted her to get better, and he would do whatever he could.

Before Adelle could answer him, there was a loud banging on the door. The whole apartment suddenly went even colder. Adelle didn't need to guess who was on the other side of the door. Grabbing Elbert, she drew him further down the hall and into the kitchen.

"It's Mr Radford again." She closed the kitchen door as quietly as she could, putting a finger to her lips at her brother. "We need to be quiet."

Elbert didn't need to be told twice. He ran into Adelle's arms and hugged her tightly, shivering with barely contained whimpers. Adelle held onto him as she heard Dean Radford's voice booming through the apartment, "Mrs Mallory! Open the door! I know you're in there!"

Nobody said anything. Adelle clutched onto her brother, silently hoping that their mother wouldn't stir. When she slept, she slept deeply. It was even deeper when Beth was unwell. Hopefully, she would know that the dreaded money lender they had been forced to go to for help was outside, demanding money yet again.

Money they didn't have.

Chapter Two
Worked to the Bone

"Fine." There was a loud huff. "I'll give you until this time tomorrow. But I'm not a patient man, Mrs Mallory. You'd better have the money."

There was a final loud thump on the door and then thundering footsteps dying away. It wasn't until she could hear nothing more of the awful man that Adelle allowed herself to breathe properly again.

"I hate that man," Elbert whispered.

"You're not the only one," Adelle murmured. She kissed his head. "Go and get some logs. I'll look after Mother. And be careful. Radford might still be around."

"Yes, Adelle."

Elbert ran out the back door, disappearing into the night with a draught coming in through the open door. Adelle shut the door and hurried back into the living room. Beth was stirring, the fire now dead. She was shivering even more, looking up at Adelle as her daughter tucked the blankets around her thin body.

"I thought I heard someone at the door," she whispered. "Who was it?"

Adelle swallowed. "There wasn't anyone at the door," she said gently. "Just go back to sleep. Elbert's gone to get some logs."

Beth managed a small smile. Then her eyes closed again.

***

Four years later:

Adelle took a look at the tray before her. The tray looked like it had seen better days. And the contents on it…that wouldn't last anyone an hour, never mind until lunchtime. But it was all they could manage.

With money being scarce, they couldn't afford to be choosy. The three of them had to get by on what they had. Even with Elbert now bringing in a wage of his own, they were barely holding their heads above water.

All Adelle could think of as she worked was that she was not going to the workhouse. That was the last stop for them. Once you went into the workhouse, it was very difficult to leave. Beth wouldn't be able to cope in there, not with how ill she was. It would kill her. Adelle wanted to avoid that place even if it meant working herself to the bone.

Picking up the tray with a heavy sigh, Adelle carried it upstairs. The small room that Beth and Adelle slept in was at the back of the apartment which meant it was always cold, even in the summer. Elbert's room was in the front, but his wasn't much better; the rooftops of the buildings across the street blocked his sunlight. Tucked away in the alley the way it was, it was practically an icebox in winter.

They couldn't live like that. But Adelle knew they didn't have a choice. This was preferable to the workhouse.

Beth was still in bed, dozing under the blankets. Her hair was spread across the pillow, and she looked so peaceful for the first time in a long time. Adelle almost burst into tears when she saw her mother sleeping. For years, Beth had been struggling with her health. There were good days and there were bad days. A lot of bad days. This was looking to be the first good day in months.

Adelle leant over and gently shook her mother's shoulder. "Mother? I've brought you breakfast. It's not much, I'm afraid."

Beth rolled over with a sigh, blinking up at her daughter. Looking at the tray, she gave a small smile and began to sit up. "Thank you, darling. I wasn't expecting this."

"I didn't want you to worry about your meal." Adelle sat on the bed and placed the tray on her mother's lap once Beth had sat up, propping herself up with the worn, beaten-down pillows. "And you need to get to work."

"I know. I'm just..." Beth sighed. "I'm so tired."

"I know. That's why I'm doing this."

Beth smiled and chucked her daughter's chin. "You're a good girl, Adelle."

"I'm glad someone thinks so."

"Don't be silly. Everyone thinks you're a good girl. My fellow teachers talk about how lovely you are, and they're delighted that you've grown up into a beautiful young woman with so much talent at her fingertips."

Adelle bit her lip to stop herself from crying. She had once been a pupil at her mother's school, and Adelle had worked hard. She wanted to do something with her life although there weren't many doors open. To hear such compliments, though, were few and far between.

"Everyone knows I'm a good girl." Adelle sighed and looked down at her hands. "And they take advantage of it. Now I'm beginning to wish I hadn't started working for myself."

In the past year, Adelle had decided she would make better money to leave her place of employment and work for herself. A few seamstresses she knew were very well-paid working on their own. Their clients were high up in Society, and the work was coming in for huge payments. They were doing very well.

Adelle, on the other hand, wasn't doing as well. She had managed to get a few clients of the lower working classes who didn't have time to do any sewing, and if they paid her properly, she would be doing quite nicely. But people in the lower classes weren't as honest, and they would do anything to get out of paying the full amount, if they paid at all. And it drove Adelle mad. She was trying to help her mother out, and her plan had been failing.

"Adelle?"

Adelle realised she had drifted off into her own thoughts. Her mother was watching her in concern. She gave Beth a small smile. "I...I'm sorry, Mother."

"There's no need to be sorry." Beth leant over and squeezed her daughter's hand. "Don't get yourself down. Everyone struggles at the beginning. You just need to persevere, and you'll get there. It takes time."

"Not like this," Adelle lamented sadly. "Everyone sees a seventeen-year-old and they believe she's going to be an easy mark. I can't begin to count how many times I've been refused payment because they claim they haven't got the money."

Adelle knew they could pay for it easily. But they just didn't want to pay a girl, someone who was too nice for her own good.

"They're a lot of fools," Beth declared. "You need to keep yourself strong, Adelle. They want you to buckle. Don't let that happen."

"I won't, Mother," Adelle vowed.

That was the last thing Adelle was going to do. She was not going to buckle under pressure. It drove her mad and gave her frequent headaches, but Adelle wasn't going to let people walk all over her. Like Beth said, it would take time.

The problem was, Adelle wasn't very patient. Dealing with people in her new business meant her patience had disappeared quite quickly.

Beth sipped at the glass of water. "Is Elbert out at work, then?"

"He should be." Adelle glanced towards her brother's closed bedroom door, which she could see across the hallway. "I don't know when he'll be back, but I'm not looking forward to cleaning his clothes later."

At fourteen, Elbert had left school and gone into work. There were lots of little menial jobs he could have done, but Elbert wanted one that would pay a lot of money. Even if it was a disgusting one. It meant he had to travel to the outskirts of London, but he did get paid relatively well as a tanner.

Even if the tannery itself absolutely stank due to everything they used to turn cow hides into leather.

"I still don't understand why dung has to be used to make leather," Beth grumbled.

"According to Elbert, it takes the bacteria away and makes the leather softer and easier to use."

"I beg to differ. It stinks the place out."

Adelle couldn't argue with that. "I don't think Elbert notices the smell anymore. At least he's earning a decent wage packet. You wouldn't want him scavenging, would you?"

"Scavengers are usually quite well paid." Beth made a face. "At least he's not a mudlark. I'd be embarrassed if he did that."

"I know. But we're not there yet, Mother." Adelle paused. "Although Elbert has spoken to me about joining the navy and building canals and tunnels."

That had Beth's face paling even more. "Oh, my goodness. Not that. That's far too dangerous, especially building tunnels. I've heard people can be killed like that."

Adelle grunted. "I'm tempted to tell him to become a legger. That should keep him quiet if his legs are exhausted."

"Oh, don't joke about that, Adelle. He's too young for that."

"He's fourteen."

"And still a child, at least in my eyes. I love him to pieces, but he doesn't understand his place in life." Beth looked close to crying. "I hope he learns to grow up soon."

Adelle didn't say anything. But she couldn't agree more. Elbert needed to grow up, or they were going to be in even more dire straits.

***

Otto Darrington was worn out. He had been arguing with his father for most of the day, and the man just wouldn't listen to reason. Otto was to put to sea the next day whether he liked it or not. Joseph Darrington wanted his son to become a merchant seaman, and he pushed Otto into it forcefully.

The man just wouldn't listen to reason. It was his way or no way. Otto hated that about the cantankerous old man. The only reason they weren't arguing now was Otto remembered he had to pick up some trousers that were being sewn up after being almost ripped to shreds. But the argument would be waiting for him when he got home.

Otto was not looking forward to that. Now his poor mother had to deal with her husband's tantrums over his son refusing to lie down and roll over when he demanded.

At least he had a brief reprieve and would get to see a pretty face. Adelle Mallory was a lovely young woman, almost like a breath of fresh air to him. Medium height and slightly built with raven hair that had a natural curl to it. And that smile of hers...it was enough to make Otto's heart skip a beat and smile in return.

The poor thing was worked far too hard, and people took advantage of her youth. But as far as Otto was aware, Adelle never complained. Otto knew her situation was dire, and yet she kept herself smiling in spite of it all. Otto had to admire that.

It was a very warm day as Otto turned into Adelle's street. Everyone seemed to be out on the road, hanging up washing, with children rushing about screaming with laughter as they played. A few of the mothers nodded and smiled at Otto as he passed. He had been along this way several times, ever since a chance encounter with another of Adelle's clients, and everyone was very friendly. The community in this area was very close knit.

Otto liked that. He liked it a lot.

Most of the windows on the buildings lining the street were open, including the apartment that Adelle lived in with her mother and brother. As Otto approached, he could hear raised voices coming from the front room. He recognised Adelle's immediately.

"Please, Mrs Daley, you need to pay for your dress."

She was trying to keep calm, but Otto could hear it in her voice: her patience was growing thin. Then another female voice, this one haughty and slightly shrill, reached his ears, "No, I won't. You did an appalling job here, Miss Mallory. I can't believe I thought you would be a good choice. Far too young and far too incompetent."

"You've had other dresses sent to me before. What's so different this time?"

The other woman sniffed. "Nothing's different on my part. Only yours. This is terrible."

Chapter Three
A Moment of Kindness

Otto sighed. He had not spoken to Adelle much, but he had a feeling that many of her clients took advantage of her youth and good nature. The lady Otto knew who told him about Adelle was not one of them. She had, however, told Otto about some other ladies who went there expecting to walk out without paying. Otto could tell Adelle was getting fed up to her teeth.

"It's exactly how I've done things before," Adelle protested. "You haven't complained about them. I got praise from you before."

"I don't know what I was thinking about that," the lady said sharply. "You're not getting a penny from me."

Otto reached the door just as it opened. A stout, buxom woman wearing nice clothes with her hair perfectly coifed was trying to leave. Then Adelle appeared behind her, grabbing at the dress in the woman's hands.

"Then you're not taking the dress, Mrs Daley," she said sharply. "Payment or no dress."

"What?" Mrs Daley started tugging. "I need this dress! It's my best dress."

"Even with my 'appalling' needlework?"

Mrs Daley bared her teeth. "It'll have to do. But I won't pay for such shoddy work."

If they fought for much longer, either Adelle was going to end up flat on her face or the fight would end up in the street. Either way, the dress was going to be ruined. Otto decided to step in. If anything, Adelle needed help. "Is there something wrong, Miss Mallory?"

Both women looked up. Then they both straightened up, both going red in the face and smoothing down their clothes. Mrs Daley gave a little giggle as she looked up at him while Adelle was trying to look anywhere but at him. Otto had to hide a smile at the sight.

"It's fine, Mr Darrington." Adelle said hurriedly. "I've got this under control."

Otto begged to differ. He turned to Mrs Daley. "What's the problem, ma'am?"

"What's the problem?" Mrs Daley held up her dress with a flourish. "This girl has no idea about sewing. She's done an appalling job on my dress."

"It's the fifth dress I've done for her." Adelle explained.

"And I wholly regret it."

Otto saw a wobble in Adelle's expression. She was close to tears. He had a sudden urge to put his arms around her and comfort her. Where had that come from? Otto focused on Mrs Daley. "Well, ma'am…"

"It's Mrs Arthur Daley," Mrs Daley simpered. "Charlotte Daley, actually."

"Mrs Daley, if you don't want to pay for what you call shoddy work, then don't." Otto neatly plucked the dress out of the woman's hands. "But you can't take the dress with you."

"What?" Mrs Daley's eyes widened, her smile fading. "But it's my dress!"

"And Miss Mallory spent many hours working on it. She gets paid for her work whether you like it or not. It's very unfair and very unkind not to pay for someone's work." Otto folded the dress over one arm, holding it away from Mrs Daley's snatching hands. "If you don't like it, don't come back to her. Clearly, you had no problems with her before, or you wouldn't keep coming back. But you must pay her, or you can leave the dress in lieu of payment."

Adelle was staring at him like she had never seen him before. Mrs Daley was beginning to realise she had been backed into a corner. Huffing loudly, she went into her purse and took out some money. Then she shoved it unceremoniously into Adelle's hands, almost making her drop it all, and held her hands out to the dress.

Otto bowed and handed it over. "There you go, Mrs Daley."

Mrs Daley scowled as she snatched the dress away. "You're lucky you have a pleasant face, young man," she grumbled. "And I'll be taking my clothes elsewhere."

Then she swept away, stalking down the road. Otto watched her go, resisting the urge to laugh. Then he turned back to Adelle, who was still staring at him. "May I come in? I believe I'm here to pick up some pants you've been working on."

"Oh." Adelle blinked. Then she shook herself and stepped aside. "Please, come in."

Otto stepped inside. He had to stop himself from shivering. It was warm outside, but inside was something else. The sun didn't seem to hit any part of the apartment even though Adelle had left the window open.

Adelle ducked past him, her head down. Even then, Otto could see her red cheeks. "You didn't need to do that," she mumbled as she went into the front room.

Otto followed her. "I did." He spread his hands. "Think of it as a knight in shining armour coming to the rescue of a fair damsel in distress."

Adelle stared at him. Then she threw her head back and laughed. That laugh was fresh and clear. It hit Otto right in the gut. "You sound like you've been reading far too much Walter Scott."

"Mother does, so I swipe them once she's finished." Otto shrugged. "I like to escape everyday life."

"I know the feeling." Adelle's smile faded. "But I wouldn't know what it really feels like. I can't remember a time when I had a day off."

"Maybe you should try it one day."

But Adelle was already shaking her head, turning away as her cheeks flushed even redder. "I'm afraid I don't have the time to read at all. I'm always working. The rent won't pay itself."

Otto had heard the situation from Adelle before, almost as if the girl was apologising for the state of her home. She had an ill mother who made herself even more ill by working, and a wayward younger brother who had had to drop out of school to start working at the young age of fourteen. Otto knew there were people worse off than his own family, but to see it like this struck him hard.

These slums were the type of places his father told him never to walk through as he would be attacked and beaten. He was better dressed than most of the inhabitants, so he would be an ideal target. But Otto couldn't bring himself to walk away, not when he saw someone like Adelle struggling.

He could see that Adelle was close to collapse. She was thin, very thin, and her complexion was pasty, her eyes sunken with exhaustion. She still looked lovely, but Otto was aware that Adelle could snap like a twig if you sneezed at the wrong moment.

"You won't do yourself any favours if you don't have a break from work," he said gently.

Adelle sighed. It was a very sad sigh. "I'm afraid I don't have a choice."

She picked up a folded pair of trousers and placed them on brown paper. Folding it over the trousers, Adelle's deft fingers used some string to tie up the parcel. Then she turned to Otto with a bright but sweet smile, one that warmed Otto as he reached out for the parcel. "Here you go, Mr Darrington. They only needed a little letting out, so the alterations weren't too bad."

Otto took the parcel, pausing when he felt his fingers brush against Adelle's. Adelle's breath hitched, and she stilled. Otto saw her eyes lifting to his, and they seemed to darken. This was getting a little too dangerous. Otto cleared his throat and drew back.

"Thank you," he mumbled. Then he managed a small smile and tucked the parcel under his arm. "Hopefully, I can walk around without showing off my stockings. Father wasn't too impressed."

Adelle giggled. It sounded a little too maniacal. "It's an interesting fashion statement, certainly."

"Not one that London likes, I'm afraid."

Otto reached into his pocket, his hand closing around the wad of money in his pocket. He knew Adelle only charged in coin, but he couldn't just walk away from her when she was clearly struggling. The softer side of him refused to let him leave without knowing Adelle was going to be all right that evening. Maybe some food, some warmth, something to keep her going.

He pulled out two large notes and held them out to her. "There's my payment for you."

"I..." Adelle stared at the money, her eyes round. "You don't need to pay that much."

"Call it gratitude for coming to my aid when I needed it."

Otto could see her still hesitating. She was going to turn him away. Taking the initiative, Otto took her hand and pressed the money into her palm, curling her fingers over it. Her hand was very cold, almost like ice. It was a startling contrast compared to how warm it was outside.

"I don't know..." Adelle began, but Otto cut her off.

"Please. Put it towards something you really need."

He wasn't going to leave until Adelle had accepted the money. From the dawning expression in her eyes, Adelle realised this. With a slight look of awe, she drew her hand back, still holding onto the money. She opened it and stared at the bills. She looked as though she was in a dream.

"Thank you, Mr Darrington."

Otto felt his throat tighten, but he swallowed and stepped back. The girl was tugging at his heart strings, and he had to leave. He was sailing the next day; nothing could come about approaching anything with Adelle Mallory.

Which was a shame because Otto wanted to stay. He wanted to help. But he had pushed his luck. Otto turned towards the door. "I'll take my leave. Good day, Miss Mallory."

His face going red, he ducked out of the apartment.

***

Adelle was still in a daze. Otto Darrington always knocked her off-balance. That gesture of kindness had completely thrown her. None of her clients had paid her that much before, and Adelle knew she couldn't accept it. But there was something about Mr Darrington...he could get her to accept the sky was red, and Adelle wouldn't be able to argue with him.

When he had first walked into her apartment three months before, asking her to alter a waistcoat and jacket for him, Adelle had been momentarily speechless. Tall, stocky, with a frame that said he was clearly a labourer, Otto Darrington cast a fine figure. Especially in Adelle's front room. Hair as black as a raven, his skin rosy brown from the sun, and dark eyes that seemed to constantly twinkle. There was something about him that Adelle felt drawn to.

Such a sweet man. Adelle didn't encounter that often. Most men wanted to give her some other payment for their goods, which Adelle flatly refused. She had been beaten before when she demanded payment, but Adelle was able to take care of herself. A few hits with the poker, and they were gone.

At least they didn't try it when Elbert was there. Adelle's little brother was not so little anymore. He had shot up in the last four years, now towering over Adelle at six feet, at least. He was turning into a man before her eyes, and Adelle could hardly believe this was the same person she had cradled in her arms as a baby when she was three years of age. Elbert Mallory was certainly very protective over his mother and sister, and he made sure the men who came to the apartment for Adelle's sewing services knew it.

He did try. He had gone through several jobs before settling on the tannery. It absolutely stank, and Elbert complained about it all the time, but it was a good job. They had no option to argue over it. Adelle had reminded him that they couldn't be choosy about jobs. They didn't want to be in the workhouse.

Just the mere mention of the word had shivers going down Adelle's spine.

Chapter Four
Desperate Times

As she worked late into the evening, aware of her mother coughing as she tried to sleep upstairs, Adelle kept looking at the clock. Where was Elbert? The tannery was on the outskirts of London, but it wasn't that far. Elbert wouldn't take long to come home.

Then again, he had been staying out later and later more recently. There were days when he wouldn't come home until it was sunrise. Adelle scolded him for that, but she never said a word to Beth. She didn't need the stress and worry about her son's nocturnal activities. Adelle was struggling with it on her own.

It was nearly ten in the evening when the door opened and closed very slowly. Adelle could hear the distinctive creak it gave when it was moved an inch at a time. Someone was trying to sneak in. And she knew who. She put aside her sewing with a heavy sigh.

"Finally!" She stood and strode into the hall. Elbert was shrugging out of his coat, dropping it onto the floor. Adelle growled at the sight, which made Elbert jump. "You're supposed to hang up your coat, Elbert. Not leave it on the floor. I'm your sister, not your slave."

Elbert turned away, grumbling. He kept his face averted from Adelle's as he swiped his coat back up off the floor and hung it up. "There," he snapped. "Satisfied?"

He tried to go past Adelle, still keeping his face turned away, but Adelle caught sight of something dark on his jaw. She grabbed his arm and swung him around.

"Leave off!"

Elbert tried to swat her away, but Adelle had already seen the damage. Elbert's face was a mess. There were bruises on his jaw, over his eye, and there was a cut above his other eye. Blood was coming from under his hairline, and his nose had been bleeding, the dried blood crusted on his mouth.

Adelle stared at him, momentarily speechless. "What...what happened to you?"

"Not your concern. It's nothing."

"Nothing!" Adelle's voice went up into a loud shrill. She hurriedly lowered it to a fierce whisper. "That is not nothing, Elbert!"

"Leave me alone, Mother," Elbert grumbled, waving her away. "I don't answer to you."

Adelle was not having that again. Her little brother had been beaten up. What on earth was going on at that tannery? She grabbed his arm, dragging him towards the kitchen.

"What?" Elbert struggled and tried to push back. "Let me go, Adelle!"

"You're coming with me right now." Adelle's fingers dug into Elbert's elbow, which made him wince. "Stop struggling, and it won't hurt as much."

She hauled her brother into the kitchen, making him sit on the stool beside the sink. Then she managed to get the last remnants of water into a bowl which she put on the table. Snatching up a cloth, Adelle lifted Elbert's head up by the chin and began to dab at the cut over his eye. Elbert flinched and tried to pull away, but Adelle swatted him over the head.

"Ouch!"

"Stop wriggling, you baby," Adelle scolded. "What do you expect?"

"A gentler touch from my big sister, perhaps?"

"You should've thought about that before you got beaten up."

Adelle was a little gentler as she cleaned the blood up. The wounds were fresh, but the blood was dry. The bruises were new. Elbert had certainly not left with them that morning. Adelle's heart ached. What on earth had happened here?

"Who did this to you, Elbert?" she asked.

Elbert's face flushed under the bruises and he averted his eyes. "A man," he mumbled.

"Are you telling me that a complete stranger dragged you into an alley and beat you up?"

"Yes. I was a link-boy for a while, remember? It happened to me all the time."

"And I would've expected you to be more vigilant about being out in the streets."

Adelle didn't believe Elbert for a minute. Her brother had never been a very good liar. He was always trying to get out of responsibilities by lying his way out, but Adelle could see straight through it. The boy was terrible at trying to be the innocent party.

"There's more going on, isn't there?"

"No!"

Adelle sighed and drew back. She was too worn out for this argument. "Elbert, don't lie to me. Now is not the time."

Elbert's face went even redder, and he looked away. When he spoke, Adelle almost didn't hear him. "I stole his watch."

Adelle thought she had misheard. She shook herself. "You...you did what?"

"I stole his watch." Elbert shrugged. "My friends and I do...a little borrowing where we can."

"Borrowing. You mean the kind of borrowing where you don't give it back?"

"We're just trying to get a bit more money for ourselves!" Elbert protested.

Adelle snorted. "How can you sell a stolen watch? No one is going to take a watch off you in exchange for money if it's clear you don't own it."

"We get something."

"You mean protection." Adelle sighed. "You fell in with that thief, Saul Lancet, didn't you?"

Elbert huffed. "Adelle, working in a tannery is disgusting. The smell is awful, and I feel sick when I'm dehairing the hides. It's a foul job. I want to do something else."

"Becoming a pickpocket isn't going to get you any further. At least you have a decent income with the tannery."

Elbert said nothing. He simply sat on his stool, scowling at the floor. Adelle had wondered if and when Elbert would fall in with the bad crowd in an attempt to get more money. Deep down, she couldn't fault him for wanting to do more. But being a pickpocket could get him arrested and put in prison. Sent to the colonies. And, in the worst-case scenario, if Elbert was in the wrong place at the wrong time, death.

Adelle didn't want that for him.

"I'm still at the tannery," Elbert grumbled. "This is just to boost the money I bring in."

"What money? You don't bring any extra money in."

"I have to do something! And it will pay off, eventually."

"When?" Adelle demanded. "After you've been caught and thrown in prison? Or after you've been killed after one too many beatings?"

Elbert shied away from her. That was when Adelle realised he was crying. Her baby brother, growing far too quickly, was crying. Tears stained his dirty cheeks. Adelle knelt before him, drawing him into a hug.

"Come here, Elbert. I don't mean to shout at you. I'm just scared you're going to get hurt."

"I'm just trying to help," Elbert mumbled.

"I know. But you need to do it sensibly." Adelle kissed his head, stroking his hair away from his face. "Mother would be devastated if she lost you."

"I know." Elbert swallowed. Then he swiped at his tears, wincing. "How is Mother?"

Adelle bit her lip. "Not good. She's still coughing away. I managed to earn enough for a loaf of bread and some firewood, but not much. She's as warm as I can get her, and I managed to get some bread in her, but..." Adelle shook her head. "She's losing her appetite."

Elbert looked like he wanted to break down. He adored his mother, and it pained Adelle to see him sobbing over his mother's ill health. Elbert looked at the ceiling. "Can I see her?"

"Once you've got yourself cleaned up." Adelle soaked the cloth again and wiped at the grime and blood on his face. "You don't want to worry her."

Elbert said nothing. There was nothing to say to that, and Adelle had no idea what to do or say to comfort him.

***

Adelle awoke with a jolt. She had just got herself to sleep when the whole room seemed to be shaking. The bed was rocking so much, Adelle was almost tipped onto the floor. She sat up and looked at her mother. Beth was coughing hard, her whole body jerking with each cough. It sounded awful.

Adelle touched her shoulder. "Mother?"

Beth looked up, her eyes taking a moment to focus on Adelle. She was pasty white, her mouth crusted dry. "I'm sorry, darling," she mumbled weakly. "I didn't mean to wake you."

"You don't need to be sorry."

"I do." Beth swallowed, licking her dry lips. "My throat feels like it's on fire. And I'm so cold." She was shivering, and all the blankets but the one Adelle had with her were wrapped around her. But she was sweating.

Adelle pressed a hand to Beth's cheek, pulling it back with a gasp. "Mother, you're burning up."

This was worse than before. Beth had been ill for a long time, but this was a turn Adelle had been dreading. There was a movement in the doorway, and Adelle looked around to see Elbert on the threshold in his nightwear. He looked scared. "Adelle?"

Adelle slid out of bed, hurrying across to her brother and pulling him into the hallway. "Get dressed," she whispered. "Go and talk to your friends. Ask the neighbours, anyone, if they can help pay for a doctor. Mother's got a fever."

"Is she…" Elbert was trembling. "Is she going to die?"

Adelle didn't know what to say to that. She cupped her brother's face. "We'll not think about that now. Just go."

Elbert didn't need to be told twice. He darted back into his room. Moments later, he was back out fully dressed without a coat and running down the stairs. Then the front door opened and slammed shut.

Adelle shivered in the cold air. It was the middle of October and still surprisingly warm outside, but that didn't get into the apartment. The apartment was still freezing, and Adelle could feel it affecting her chest as well. She could only hope it didn't hit her hard as well. That was not what they needed now. Not when Beth was seriously ill. Nobody else could afford to be sick with her.

"Adelle?"

Adelle hurried back to her mother's side. "I'm here, Mother."

"I…" Beth licked her lips again. "I'm sorry for putting you to so much trouble."

"Oh, Mother." Adelle sat on the bed. "I wish you wouldn't keep apologising. It's not your fault that you're not well."

"I've been ill for years. But never like this." Beth coughed again. It sounded worse than before. "I can't afford to be off from work and sick. The children..."

"Are just going to get sicker themselves if you go into the school." Adelle cut off. "And you're not well enough to look after yourself, never mind them. You need to rest. The more you rest, the quicker you'll get better."

That had been their mantra for a long time. But now Adelle was beginning to hate it. Beth rested as much as she could, and it never seemed to work. It just made her worse.

Beth raised her other hand, her trembling fingers brushing against Adelle's cheek. "You're putting too much on your shoulders, Adelle," she said weakly.

"I can handle it, Mother."

But Beth was shaking her head. "No, you can't. You're far too young to become a de facto mother to Elbert."

"Would you stop talking like that?" Adelle clasped her mother's other hand. "You're not going to die. Just...just sleep. Talking's not doing you any good."

Beth didn't argue. Her breathing still raspy, she closed her eyes. Soon, she was fast asleep. She was still sweating, but she was shivering enough to make all the blankets move. Adelle adjusted the blankets a little, so her mother could cool down. Then she lay beside Beth, stroking her hair. It was something Beth had done when Adelle was a little girl and had nightmares. She would cuddle Adelle as she settled down and stroked her hair, singing a little lullaby. Adelle wasn't about to sing, however. She couldn't; she would end up crying again.

Chapter Five
Death Never Becomes the End

After what seemed like an age, the door opened and closed again. Adelle could hear footsteps, these slower, coming up the stairs. She jumped up and hurried into the hallway, meeting Elbert as he reached the top of the stairs.

"Anything?" Even before she said it, Adelle could see her brother's face.

He shook his head. "Nothing. Nobody can afford the local doctor. They're very sorry for us and will help with what they can, but they can't pay for a doctor."

Adelle's heart sank. It had been worth a try, but everyone was in the same situation. The doctor, who was supposed to help the poor, was far too dear for any of them. It was illogical, but it was there. She squared her shoulders, trying not to cry. "Go and get her some water. We need to keep her cool."

Looking like he was close to tears himself, Elbert nodded. Then he set off back down the stairs.

***

Beth didn't last the week. She was dead three days later. Adelle woke up in the morning to find her mother's cold body beside her. She didn't know how to react; every part of her was numb. Deep down, she had known Beth would die soon. But Adelle tried to deny it for a long time. She didn't want to believe it. Her mother was strong. She had lasted this long.

Now she was no more.

Adelle had sent Elbert, who was crying hard when he saw his mother's body, to tell the doctor. He was the one who arranged for people to take away dead bodies. At least that didn't cost anything, which left a nasty taste in Adelle's mouth.

The doctor was over promptly, four men in tow. They wrapped up Beth's body after she had been checked over, and then they carried her out to the wagon they had brought with them. Adelle stood in the doorway and watched as her mother was slung onto the cart like a hunk of meat.

The doctor turned to her, touching his hat with his fingers. "My sincere condolences, Miss Mallory," he said solemnly. "If only you had called me. I had no idea Mrs Mallory was this ill."

Adelle couldn't stop herself. "If you would lower your prices to something we could have been able to afford, Mother might be alive right now."

The doctor's expression hardened. Then it went blank. He grunted and spun away sharply, stalking towards the wagon. After he climbed up onto the front, the wagon was driven away. People had come out from their lodgings and were watching the death wagon roll past. Several people made the sign of the cross. Others were crying. Adelle wanted to cry herself, but she couldn't. Nothing would happen.

She went back inside, not wanting to see everyone watching her with pity. Elbert was sitting in the front room, curled up against the wall and rocking, his head on his knees. He was sobbing quietly. Adelle's heart broke at the sight. She went over to him. "Elbert?"

"I miss her, Adelle." Elbert looked up. His face was streaked with tears. "I miss her, and she's only just gone."

"I know." Adelle sat beside him, gathering her brother against her side. "I miss her, too. But we'll manage. We always do."

"We can't manage without Mother."

Adelle said nothing. She knew it would be tough, and she had no idea how they were going to cope without their mother. But they had to; they had no choice.

"My, what a touching scene."

Adelle started. A tall, lean man with oily red hair was in the doorway, his hat in his hand along with a long black cane. He was dressed like he had just come from a funeral. Adelle's heart sank. Not now. They couldn't be dealing with him as well.

"Mr Radford." Adelle managed to stand, Elbert jumping to his feet beside her. "What are you doing here?"

"The door was open, and I saw your mother's body being brought out." Dean Radford shrugged. "I knew someone had to be here."

Of course he would be watching the apartment. The money lender was determined to get his money back. Beth had never said how much she had borrowed from him, and Adelle didn't really want to know. It had to be a large amount if Radford was still loitering about. But to ask them now? It was despicable.

"We didn't invite you in," Elbert snapped.

Radford snickered. "I don't take orders from children."

"You will this time," Adelle snapped. "Our mother has just died! We're not in the mood for any kind of conversation."

"Touching. I want my money, and I will have it now." Radford shrugged. "Or by the end of the week. Give you time for some mourning."

"How very thoughtful," Adelle sneered. She shook her head. "Take a look around. We haven't got any money."

"You need to pay it somehow. Maybe sell some of your things."

"Not a chance!" Elbert shouted.

Radford snorted. "Well, twenty pounds is not going to come out of thin air, is it?"

That had Adelle freezing. Elbert gasped. Radford looked smug at the thought of shocking them.

Adelle swayed. "Twenty pounds?"

"That's how much your mother owed." Radford smirked. "Large sum, isn't it? And you need to pay it, Miss Mallory. You're her next of kin."

Twenty pounds was more than Adelle made in a year. When her clients paid. If they didn't, Adelle couldn't even make five pounds. Radford had to know that.

"You're a snake," she hissed.

"I'm just doing my job." Then his eyes drifted over Adelle. "However, there may be another arrangement we can come to..."

"Not a chance."

Adelle would never go down that road. Never. Radford's smirk disappeared, and he scowled. Then he tapped his cane sharply on the floor. "End of the week. Twenty pounds. Or I come get it by force. I'm not above raising my hand to children."

Elbert stepped forward, hands clenched at his sides. "Just try it," he snarled.

Radford looked at him thoughtfully. Then he chuckled. "You've got some courage, I'll give you that, Master Mallory." He touched his hat again. "Miss Mallory."

Then he was gone, not bothering to close the door behind him.

***

Adelle was exhausted. Her stomach was growling, and her fingers were sore. All she wanted to do was get home and go to bed. She was too tired for anything else.

Just one more job and then Adelle could leave.

The past six months had been painful. Losing her mother in October had been one of the most difficult things Adelle thought could happen. Then the debt had been thrown on them. Adelle and Elbert had no idea what to do about the twenty pounds needed to repay Radford. Their furniture wouldn't sell for much, if anything at all, and Adelle wouldn't be able to get that money in a week from her work.

Thankfully, they had received a kind offer. One that completely blindsided Adelle. Elbert's boss at the tannery had come forward. He had heard of the debt and their mother's death and offered to pay it without any talk about paying him back. Adelle, proud as she was, tried to refuse it, but he was insistent. Adelle was able to pay off Radford, who looked almost disappointed that he wouldn't have to get the money by force.

Elbert's boss also helped out with the funeral, asking a few favours. Adelle almost cried when she was told that everything had been sorted out for her. She had never known such kindness. Her neighbours grouped together and brought her a mourning dress as well as mourning clothes for Elbert. It had nearly caused Adelle to have a breakdown.

But she couldn't. Elbert needed her. They needed money to survive. That was when another proposition came in. The older brother of a neighbour worked on the docks, and he said he had a room to rent if they needed it. In return, he offered a discount on the rent if Elbert would work for him in whatever capacity he could. Elbert was eager to accept, wanting something that didn't stink as much as the tannery.

Adelle had been a bit more dubious. There had to be a catch somewhere. Surely there was. But they had no choice; they couldn't afford to live where they had been born and raised. They had to leave.

So they had moved into the rooms at the docks. It was a decent size and was a little warmer than their home, seeing as it was practically backed up to the boiler room of the factory next door. It did smell of fish, but it was better than animal dung.

Elbert had started working on the docks, helping with the various ships as they came in and out, carrying goods around and other tasks. He seemed to be enjoying himself, even in the middle of winter when it was freezing cold. But he didn't complain. Adelle wondered if he had been worked too hard to complain, too tired to whine about his workload.

However, it did look as though he was enjoying it. It didn't pay much, just about as much as the tannery had, but Elbert threw himself into everything.

Adelle, on the other hand, was feeling gloomy. Her small business wasn't going to go well over here at all. She couldn't carry on, and it had left her practically destitute. She needed to get a job again, which she found two streets over in a clothing factory. Adelle became one of the many girls who sewed dresses for the upper-classes once the cloth and other finer materials came off the machine. That Adelle didn't mind – she had been doing that for years – but it was less pay than before and soon the work became monotonous. All Adelle could think of now was the factory. She was stuck in the same continuous cycle.

It paid the rent – just – but not much else. Adelle could feel herself getting thinner and thinner, her clothes close to falling off her slight frame. She was going to fall over and snap in half if this carried on.

Maybe she should speak to a few men who worked on the docks, ask if they needed any clothes mended. The dockers and sailors were better at paying people for their services, and they were very kind to her and her brother. They would appreciate someone looking out for them.

If their wives didn't object that is. Adelle had come across several jealous women since moving to the docks, especially when she turned eighteen the month before. They considered her a threat, which amused Adelle. As if she would be considered a threat to any woman. Not with the way she was.

It was pitch black outside, the candles almost going out, when Adelle finally finished. She was one of the last ones there, a few younger girls still sewing frantically. One of them was almost in tears. Adelle tidied her workstation and went to the end of the room, curtsying to her supervisor.

"I've finished, Mrs Langley. Goodnight."

"Goodnight, Adelle." The haughty lady barely looked up as she wrote away in her huge ledger. "Make sure you're in bright and early."

"I will be," Adelle promised.

More than likely, she would be back in a few hours. Adelle now had a problem with sleeping. She would fall asleep for three or four hours, wake up, and be unable to get back to sleep. She was going to be in before anyone else as usual.

This was going to kill her one day. Adelle wouldn't be surprised if she dropped dead by the end of the year.

She left the factory side door and headed down the alley. Her journey wasn't long at all, just turn left twice and then she was outside her rooms. Elbert would be home by now, his hours a little more regular than hers. He would be snoring away, which would also keep Adelle awake.

Another sleepless night. That was all she needed. And Adelle was not looking forward to it.

Chapter Six
A Chance Encounter

She was jerked out of her thoughts when she almost bumped into a body that came out of the shadows. Hands reached out to steady her, fingers tightening on her arms.

"Well, what do we have here?" came a drawl above her head. "A pretty sight, I must say."

Adelle could smell the stench of alcohol. It was pungent, and it made her stomach churn. She tried to step away. "Let me go."

Then she heard someone behind her. Looking over her shoulder, Adelle saw someone else, his face half-bathed in darkness. He was swaying a little. "Why? We're on our way to a pub." His yellow teeth flashed in the moonlight. "Fancy coming with us?"

"No, thank you." Adelle winced as the grip on her arms tightened. "Let me go."

"Now, come on." The first man spun her around, pressing her against his chest. "That's not very nice."

"Get away from me!" Adelle kicked back, striking his shin. The grip around her waist slackened a little, and Adelle turned. She punched him on the nose, the action jarring her arm and making her hand sting. Something broke under her fist, and Adelle saw the brigand stagger back, clutching his nose. When his hands came away, there was blood everywhere. There was a chuckle behind Adelle. "She's got you there, Charlie."

Charlie snarled. "You're going to pay for that, you little chit." He lunged at her.

Adelle dodged sideways, ducking under his friend as he reached for her. Then she ran. If she could get to the docks, there would have to be someone who would help her. Her heart in her mouth, Adelle ran out of the alley, almost tripping over her skirts.

Then she ran into someone. A solid, large body that grabbed at Adelle as she lost her balance. Adelle screamed and tried to fight back but found herself being held even tighter.

"Whoa, take it easy!"

Adelle froze. That voice. She knew it. A voice from long past. Adelle looked up and gasped.

Otto Darrington was holding her, staring down at her in confusion. Then his eyes widened when he recognised her. "Miss Mallory?"

He looked different from the year before. His jaw was dusted with dark bristles and his skin was even more brown. But his eyes...they hadn't changed.

Adelle was shaken out of her reverie by the sound of shouting behind her. Otto frowned and looked behind her.

Adelle grabbed at his lapels. "Please," she pleaded desperately. "Help me."

Otto nodded and set her behind him as Charlie and his friend came into the street.

Charlie's face was still bloody, his nose clearly going the wrong way. He snarled at Otto. "Get lost! We saw her first!"

"Clearly, she didn't like what she saw," Otto drawled. "The lady said to leave her alone. I could hear it down the street."

"She's a hellion," the second thug hissed. "She broke Charlie's nose."

"Are you going to stand there whining, or are you going to leave the lady be?"

Charlie snorted. "She's no lady, I'm sure of that." He started towards Adelle.

Adelle whimpered and shrank back, only to see Otto take a step forward. He squared up to Charlie, his body language saying he was ready for a fight.

"You want to try it?" Otto said quietly. "Because I guarantee I'll knock you flat on your back."

Charlie hesitated. He took one long look at Adelle, who felt a shiver of cold go down her spine. Then he turned away with a grunt, shaking his head at his friend. "Come on, Mickey. They're not worth it."

Adelle sagged in relief as they walked away back into the alley. She swayed, only to be caught by Otto. She hadn't realised that he had moved.

"Miss Mallory?" Otto cupped her face in his hands, gently turning her head one way and then the other. "Are you hurt? They didn't harm you, did they?"

"No. I didn't give them the chance." Adelle's mouth felt dry. Her heart was going at double the time with Otto touching her like this. She licked her lips and managed a smile. "Thank you for rescuing me, Mr Darrington."

Otto smiled. And Adelle had to bite back a sigh. That smile was still enough to make her weak-kneed.

"I'm glad you remember me." Otto said warmly.

"I could hardly forget you after your kindness to me." Adelle then realised Otto was still holding onto her, and his hands were very warm. She cleared her throat and drew back, smoothing her hands on her skirts. "But…I thought you were at sea. You said you were going to British Guiana in the Caribbean."

"I came back a few weeks ago." Otto made a face. "Hopefully, that will be the one and only time I go to sea."

"Why? I thought British Guiana was a beautiful place."

"It is. But I get seasick. Being on a boat didn't do any good for me."

Adelle stared. Then she burst out laughing.

"What?"

"A merchant seaman gets seasick? Why did you become a sailor, then, if it makes you sick?"

Otto sighed. "My father insisted. Said I needed to learn from the bottom, and that means going to sea, just like he did." He paused. "Are you heading home?"

"Pardon?" Then Adelle remembered why they were there. "Yes. Yes, I am."

"Would you like me to walk you back, then?" Otto shook his head. "You shouldn't be out in these streets on your own. Especially when your apartment is in the other direction."

"We…we don't live there anymore." Adelle bit her lip. She would not cry now. She would not. "My brother and I live around the corner now at the docks backing onto the factory."

"You what?" Otto blinked. "What happened to the apartment? And what about your mother?"

"Mother..." Adelle took a deep breath, folding her hands in front of her. "She died last autumn. Elbert and I couldn't afford the apartment, and we were lucky enough to get what we could."

Otto stared. Then his face seemed to darken in the moonlight, and he shuffled from foot to foot. "Oh. Forgive me. I had no idea."

"You don't need to apologise. You didn't know." Adelle could feel tears about to fall. She squared her shoulders, trying not to waver. Falling apart in front of a man was not good conduct in public. "I would like to go home now."

"Of course." Otto shook himself and held out his arm. "I'll escort you."

Adelle stared at his arm. She had never been offered an escort before, and no man had offered his arm to her. It felt incredibly strange. But Adelle slipped her hand into the crook of his elbow and fell into step beside Otto as they walked towards the docks. As they walked along, Adelle gave Otto a sidelong glance. He looked older, more grown up than before. More handsome than she remembered. He seemed to be bigger, filling out more. Clearly, he had been working hard, and it was beginning to show. Otto looked more like a seaman, even in his smart evening clothes.

But Adelle still had a moment of feeling lightheaded when she saw him. He still had an effect on her. And Adelle had no idea what that could mean.

Otto glanced at her, and Adelle saw his expression softening.

"How are you holding up?" he asked.

"I beg your pardon?"

"With your mother's death. I see you're not wearing your mourning clothes."

Adelle winced. "I would still be wearing them today, had they not fallen apart on me. Even with my ministrations to mend it, the dress just collapsed."

"I thought it was a little short." Otto winced. "That was disrespectful. Forgive me."

"Besides, I haven't got time to mourn. Not when I have rent to pay." Adelle made a face. "I work in a clothing factory. They make the cloth, and I'm one of the girls who sews the garments together. Most of the clothes go towards the theatre industry. The work is incredibly long and barely pays."

"Why do you do it, then? What happened to your working from home?"

"That left me almost destitute. I had to do something else, or I was going to end up doing something I despised." Like going into the workhouse. But Adelle didn't want to say that out loud.

"It sounds like you're doing too much." Otto sounded concerned.

Adelle frowned. "I feel like I'm doing too much, yes, but who else is going to pay the rent? Elbert's job on the docks pays some, but it doesn't cover everything. It's not enough."

It would never be enough. Even though the rent was lower than before – much lower – Adelle struggled to pay her end. While their new landlord was more sympathetic, he wouldn't allow it to go on for long.

Otto was still frowning at her. He shook his head. "You shouldn't have to live like that."

"I know that." Adelle shuddered. "But we haven't got a choice. I'd rather be doing this than the workhouse."

"You don't think it's that bad, do you?"

"I think it will be if we can't keep it up." Adelle gestured at their surroundings. "This is my home now. And that's where I live, right there."

She pointed at the second floor above a fishmonger's shop on the corner of the street. The smell of fish was palpable even from where they were. In the winter, climbing those stone steps when they were iced over wasn't fun, but it was the only way into the rooms they used. Adelle had to call it home; she had no other choice about it.

They were silent as they walked to the shop. On the pavement, right by the small alleyway Adelle had to go down before she climbed the steps, Otto stopped and turned to her. He didn't look happy.

"I feel reluctant about leaving you like this. What if those thugs come back?"

"I'll be fine. They won't hurt me. Mr Lawley, the fishmonger, is a fierce man. He won't let me get hurt." Adelle blinked up at him. "Why should you be so concerned about my welfare, anyway?"

They were standing a little too close. If they were in public, Adelle would have been chastised. It wasn't proper at all. But Adelle couldn't bring herself to pull away. Otto stared down at her, his eyes piercing.

"Because I'd like to think that I'm a gentleman," he answered softly. "I want to be considered one. And," he added, his face going a little red, "I think it's safe to say that I'm quite taken with you."

Adelle's mouth fell open. "You like me? But..."

Otto held up a hand, cutting her off. "Don't try to deflect. I can tell what you're going to do, so please don't." He lowered his hand, his gloved fingers brushing over Adelle's cheek. Even with the gloves on, his hands were very warm. "May I see you again? I would very much like to."

Adelle felt like she had fallen into a dream world. A man like Otto Darrington wanted to see her again? It couldn't be true, could it?

But the sudden wind that whipped around them, causing Adelle to sway into Otto as she lost her balance, told her that this was very real. Otto was really there, and he really wanted to see her again. Adelle gasped and pushed away, clasping her hands. Otto gave her a bemused look.

"Am I that much of an ogre?"

"No!" Adelle blushed and looked at the ground. "Most certainly not. I'm...I'm just a little overwhelmed. No man has asked to see me again."

"Then they clearly haven't looked closely at you and seen what I have." Otto smiled. "Which means I don't have to challenge anyone for a duel."

Chapter Seven
A Glimpse of Happiness

"A duel? We're not in the last century."

Otto laughed. That deep, rumbling laugh had Adelle shivering all over. What was happening to her? She shook herself and tried to gather her thoughts.

"All right, Mr Darrington. I don't have a day off for a while, but you can walk me home again, if you wish."

"Of course." Otto's eyes seemed to glow in the dark. "Same time tomorrow night?"

"Yes. Down that alley I came out of."

"I'll be there." Otto took her hand and lifted it to his mouth, kissing her fingers. "Goodnight, Miss Mallory."

Adelle could barely stutter out her goodnights before Otto lowered her hand and walked away, crossing the road while he whistled a jolly tune. She stared after him, waiting for reality to come back and tell her it was a cruel misunderstanding.

Maybe the cruel reality was to delay the inevitable. But Adelle wanted to make the most of it.

***

Otto felt like God had been smiling down on him. While he had been at sea, Otto had thought about Adelle. She was what kept him going, helping him on those nights when he couldn't sleep due to his stomach. That smile of hers and that sweet voice had Otto feeling better about himself.

It got him through several tough times at sea.

He had planned to look for her when he got back the previous month, but his father had decided that keeping his son closer to home and working on the docks shifting goods around in his warehouse would keep him busy. Otto didn't mind — he preferred working in the warehouses than on ships — but his fellow workers didn't let him forget that he was the boss's son. Otto hated that part. He just wanted to be one of the workers, a normal person.

That wasn't going to happen when he had a father like Joseph Darrington.

At least he had been able to go out for the evening with his parents. Sarah Darrington had been the one to suggest they go to the theatre. Otto had been enthusiastic, but not his father. The two of them had started arguing shortly after the final curtain, and Otto had left for a long walk. He needed to calm down before he went home, or the argument would get more volatile.

Otto had a temper like his father. And he wasn't afraid to have a fight even if his father would beat him black and blue. His mother didn't need to see that. She shouldn't have to witness such awful behaviour.

Seeing Adelle Mallory had lifted his spirits even if she was running from a couple of thugs with bad intentions. Otto was surprised to see her on the docks, but he wasn't going to question it much. This felt like a special message for him, one that Otto wasn't going to alter.

Having Adelle agree to see him again had his heart feeling lighter. Otto ended up whistling all the way home. The household maid, Harriet, opened the door to Otto's knock and was surprised at his jovial manner. Otto handed her his coat and hat before heading towards the stairs.

A sharp voice barking from the front room stopped Otto on the bottom step. "Where have you been?"

Otto sighed. His parents were still up. Bracing himself, he went into the room. The fire was burning brightly, and his mother was sitting beside it doing her sewing.

His father was sitting in his usual armchair, an open book on his lap. He glowered at Otto over his spectacles. "I asked you a question, boy," he snapped. "Where have you been?"

Otto put his hands behind his back, linking his fingers tightly together. It was better than taking a swing at his father. "I went out for a walk," he said evenly. "I needed to clear my head."

His father snorted. "You're too hot-headed for your own good, Otto."

"Where do you think I got it from?"

Sarah winced and glanced at her husband.

Darrington sat forward, his eyes almost like black beads as he surveyed his son. "Don't talk back to me, boy," he growled. He sat back with a shake of his head. "I bet you were with some girl getting up to trouble."

"You make it sound like I go around with women all the time."

"What else am I supposed to think?"

"Father, I would never be so disrespectful."

"I hope not." Darrington waved a hand at his wife. "Your mother would certainly not approve."

Sarah lowered her sewing and gave her husband a cool look. "Unlike you, Joseph, I respect and trust our son," she said. "He's not a fool."

"I didn't ask for you to comment," Darrington shot at her.

Otto gritted his teeth. His mother had put up with a lot in the twenty-five years they had been married. "Don't talk to Mother like that, Father. She doesn't deserve it."

"Keep your mouth shut." Darrington stretched out his legs towards the fire with a heavy sigh. "That feels nice. By the way, we need to discuss when you're going back out."

"Back out where?" Otto stared. "You mean back out to sea? I thought we agreed just on the one trip and that was it."

"You agreed to one trip. I didn't." Darrington pointed out. "You do as you're told."

Otto couldn't believe his ears. He had mentioned in the past that he wanted to follow in his father's footsteps – that was partly true, he did find the docks his home – but Otto refused to go back out to sea again. Especially after the awful trip previously. Otto was surprised that he wasn't still tormented about his constant sickness and fainting spells. Sea air wasn't good for him at all. "I'm a terrible sailor, Father! Surely you were told about that by my captain."

"I was, but you were always trying to find a way to get out of things. At least in the middle of the ocean, you couldn't get off that ship." His father put his book aside and took off his spectacles. "You were also a competent sailor but very surly."

"Can you imagine why? I was sick all the time."

"That can be rectified. You're a worker they need right now. And you're going."

Otto looked at his mother. She had protested as much as Otto had when Darrington decided to send Otto to sea, but the thick-headed old fool hadn't paid her any attention. Sarah looked just as shocked as her son.

"If Otto doesn't want to go, Joseph," she protested, "he doesn't have to. He's a grown man, not a little boy we can shove around."

"Being a merchant seaman means a good wage," Darrington pointed out.

Otto snorted. "A good wage? Have you been to sea lately?"

Darrington growled and stood. He towered over his son. "I'm not having your protests anymore, Otto. You'll do as you're told."

There was going to be no way to sway this man. Otto knew how stubborn Joseph Darrington could be. Arguing with him right now was not going to be useful. Otto would have to bide his time. Hopefully, he wouldn't be going anytime soon. From what he knew of the ships in dock, none of them were leaving in the near future. For now, Otto was safe.

He just didn't know for how long. Sighing heavily, Otto turned towards the door. "I'm going to bed." He then turned back and kissed his mother on the head. "Goodnight, Mother."

"Goodnight, dear."

"Don't think that's going to get you out of this conversation," Darrington warned.

Otto resisted the urge to roll his eyes as he turned away. "Of course not, Father. I wouldn't dream of it."

***

Adelle wasn't quite sure what she had been thinking when she agreed to meet Otto Darrington again. What could he possibly see in her? The two of them were from different stations in life, not compatible at all. And yet...

Adelle found herself smiling whenever she thought of the handsome young seaman. He had changed in the year since they had last seen each other, and Adelle liked the change. Otto seemed more world-wise, more... She wasn't sure how to describe it, but she liked it.

Perhaps it was that which made her agree to see him again. Or perhaps it was because she needed something to lift her spirits. Otto had the ability to do that, and Adelle realised that he was right. She needed to look after herself for once in her life. Instead of focusing on her brother and everything else weighing her down, Adelle needed to do something for her.

This was for her. And her heart swelled every time she was in Otto's company. He was a gentleman and very attentive. They didn't do much beyond going for walks or having dinner in a local restaurant, but Adelle didn't care. This was the first time a man had chosen to see her as someone they wanted to take out, to court. And it felt like heaven.

Adelle didn't want it to stop.

It carried on like that for three months as spring turned into summer. And Adelle felt lighter than before. She didn't mind going to the factory and working herself down to the bone. She didn't mind being in small dwellings and having to pay rent that took all her money. Just knowing that Otto was there when she needed someone to talk to made everything feel better for Adelle.

On her only day off in the two weeks in the middle of July, Adelle headed towards the small park that was near the docks. The smell of fish was not as noticeable here, and it was picturesque. There was a lot of foot traffic and several of the middle-to-upper classes came out this way to go riding. It didn't matter what social class you were, there was always someone here to touch their forelock and greet you. It was one of Adelle's favourite places.

She hovered under the usual tree she and Otto met at, looking out over the small lake spread out beside her. Ducks were swimming about happily, quacking away and chasing each other across the water. There had been times when she and Otto would sit under the tree simply to talk and watch the ducks. Otto seemed to be just as content as Adelle. That smile of his never seemed to fade. Adelle was glad it didn't. She liked seeing it.

Then Adelle's attention was caught by a couple across the water under another tree. They were sitting together against the trunk, the woman snuggled up to the man. They were holding each other, kissing every few moments. Even across the lake, Adelle could see them smiling. It was a sweet sight, even with their chaperone in the shape of a doughy-faced woman sitting nearby.

Adelle didn't know she had company until someone started tickling her from behind. She squealed and tried to get away, but that only resulted in her being captured in someone's arms and falling sideways. Familiar laughter sounded above her, and Adelle rolled over to see Otto laughing, his eyes twinkling as he looked at her.

"Otto!" Adelle slapped his chest before shifting off him. "Don't do that! You frightened me."

"I'm sorry. I thought you knew I was there."

"I didn't." Adelle nodded across the lake. "I was watching them."

Otto sat beside her. He looked as though he had just come from work, still wearing his overalls from when he worked in the warehouses. The smell of fish still clung to him. "Shouldn't you be averting your gaze like a good girl and giving them privacy?"

"I can't help it, not when it's in front of me." Adelle sighed. "It's such a sweet sight."

"It is sweet, but I think they would prefer no prying eyes."

"Then they shouldn't do that in public. Even if they have a chaperone."

Otto laughed. Then he rose to his feet, holding out a hand. "Come on. Let's go for a walk."

Chapter Eight
Threat of Separation

Adelle took his hand and allowed Otto to bring her to her feet. Then he tucked her hand into the crook of his arm as they walked along the bank of the lake. Two people, a young man and woman on horseback, went past them. They nodded greetings to them, which Adelle returned. Otto did but only after a hesitation.

Adelle peered up at him. There was something off about him today. Normally he was jovial and light, unable to stop talking or smiling. But now the smile was fading a little, and there was a frown between his eyes. Adelle wanted to reach up and rub the frown away. This was not like Otto at all. She prodded him in the side.

Otto winced. "Ouch! What did you do that for?"

"Because you were away in dreamland," Adelle shot back. "Are you all right, Otto?"

"I..." Otto hesitated. Then he looked away. "I'm perfectly all right."

"Don't lie to me. I know there's something wrong."

"I'm not lying to you."

Adelle sighed. She couldn't tolerate Otto lying to her. That had happened too many times by other people for her to count. She stopped, Otto stopping with her.

He turned, frowning at her. "Adelle?"

"I thought we agreed if we were going to see each other that we shouldn't keep secrets. Secrets aren't good for anything." Adelle tugged at his arm. "Now, tell me, please. What's wrong?"

For a moment, she thought Otto was going to brush it aside. But he didn't. He ran a hand through his hair, which seemed longer than before. It was a good look on him. "Father's been driving me mad, that's all," Otto finally said.

Adelle sighed. Joseph Darrington again. That man was fierce and cruel. He was also a taskmaster who expected the best from his workers. Adelle couldn't fault him for that, but she didn't like the way Darrington treated his son. Otto was getting frustrated with the way his father was pressuring him into doing things he wanted to avoid. He vented to Adelle about it, and Adelle didn't know what to do except just be there whenever Otto wanted someone to talk to.

It made her feel a little helpless, something she didn't like at all.

"What's Mr Darrington done now?"

"He's still trying to get me onto a ship," Otto grumbled. "He...he wants me to go to India."

Adelle gasped. "India? That's a long way, isn't it?"

"A very long way. Failing that, the Caribbean again. Or even Australia. As long as I'm on a ship, he doesn't care." This had been the same thing for the past three months. Darrington seemed to be determined to get rid of his son.

"I would have thought a father would want their son close by to learn the business."

"I thought so, too. And I wouldn't mind learning the import business myself. It's very fruitful right now, and it's something I prefer to do. But Father…" Otto shook his head. "He wants me to be a merchant seaman, just like he was when he was my age."

"And you don't want to?"

"Adelle, I get seasick. I don't mind working near the water, but once the floor starts swaying, that's when things change." Otto started walking again, Adelle hurrying to catch up before falling into step beside him. "Father just won't listen to reason. I get beaten by the other sailors, who think it's amusing that I'm reduced to a quivering wreck when I'm on a rolling boat."

"You can't live like that, Otto," Adelle protested. "It's going to kill you one day. If the sailing doesn't, your fellow sailors will."

"What can I do about it, though? It's not as if I can go to Father and ask to stay here. He won't listen."

Chances were, the two of them would get into a shouting argument, one that could turn physical. Otto could tamp down on his temper, but not when it came to his father. They seemed like chalk and cheese but were actually so much alike that neither would willingly admit it.

She shook his arm, making him stop again. Adelle stepped in front of him, cupping his clean-shaven jaw in her hands. "You don't know until you try. I did that yesterday with Mrs Langley. She was very surprised when I offered her a proposition, and I didn't back down."

"A proposition?" Otto frowned. "What did you do?" Adelle saw the light dawning in his eyes. "You asked for more work, didn't you?"

"I asked if she could get me to work the night shifts. They actually pay more, practically double what I earn during the day."

"That's because nobody wants to work the night shift in there."

"Exactly. Mrs Langley was very surprised that I even asked to do that as everyone else had to be forced." Adelle hurried on as she saw Otto's expression. "It's just to give me a few more pennies so I can pay rent and be able to eat. And then I'll have my days free."

But Otto still didn't look happy. "You're burning the candle at both ends, Adelle. You're going to collapse."

"I've never needed much sleep." Adelle brushed his concerns aside. "I'll mange. And I told you, Elbert and I need the rent."

Otto looked pained. He ran his fingers into Adelle's hair, resting his forehead against hers with a heavy sigh. "You shouldn't have to live like that," he said. "I've told you before. And what about your brother?"

"He's bringing in what he can, but after paying rent, we have nothing."

"Can't you ask the landlord to lower the rent?"

"That is the lowered rent. He's not willing to go any further. This money would be what we need for food, for wood for the fire. When winter comes along, we're going to need it."

Adelle didn't like the idea of working at night – she had a tendency to fall asleep as soon as it got dark – but it would work out better for them in the long run. At least she had days when she could sleep. She had gotten used to the sounds of the docks; once she was asleep, it was tough to wake her up. Elbert could vouch for that.

Then Adelle realised Otto was digging into his pocket. He drew out a slim wallet which he opened. Adelle saw a few notes in there, almost bursting out of the wallet. Otto took out some money and held it out to her. "Take it."

"What?"

"I've told you that I'd happily help you if you let me. Take it."

But Adelle was already shaking her head. "No, Otto. I can't. We've been through this before."

"You can take it."

"I really can't." Adelle pushed his hands back. "I don't like asking people for money. It has to come from me and me alone. Just...don't ask me again. It's your money, not mine."

Otto looked as though he was going to argue. Then he sighed and put his money away, slipping his wallet into his pocket. "All right. I won't." He kissed her forehead. "But it's there if you ever need it."

It wasn't the first time Otto had offered her money. The only time Adelle had accepted had been when she was working for herself. Not anymore. Once was enough. Adelle felt like she was going to cry over Otto's kindness. "I don't deserve someone like you," she said.

Otto smiled. He kissed her forehead again before drawing her into his arms, hugging her against his chest. "You, my sweet Adelle, certainly deserve it. And don't believe otherwise." He took her hand and kissed it, still smiling at her. "Come, let's take a walk. We haven't got long before I have to get back."

Adelle wasn't about to argue with that.

***

Otto thought Adelle was mad for working the night shifts. From what he had heard, they were tough and dangerous. But he had to admire her for taking that step; she was proactive that much he could agree with. She did whatever she could to keep her and her brother safe.

Otto loved her tenacity.

It hadn't taken much. The more time he spent with Adelle, the more Otto fell in love with her. She was a kind girl, very sweet and very proud. She made him smile whenever they were together. Otto couldn't ask for anyone better.

Otto had made up his mind a long time ago. He was going to marry Adelle. She would become his wife by the end of the year. They would find a place of their own, and Otto would be able to look after both her and Elbert. The boy had a good heart and was fiercely protective of his sister, and he and Otto had a strong amount of respect for each other. His approval was all Otto needed.

There was just one problem, though, and that was his current situation. Otto knew his father wanted him at sea again, but he didn't know when. Otto didn't like the uncertainty, so he needed to take action. Adelle had managed to do it for herself, and it had worked. Now Otto needed to take a page from her book and do the same.

Maybe his father would respect him for being more proactive.

There was only one way to find out.

Otto made his way up to his father's office in the warehouse. He could hear his father's voice booming out the window above, shouting at the workers in the yard as they fumbled with the goods. Otto had been shouted at himself, but he was able to grit his teeth and ignore it. It was work, and he was an employee, not the boss's son.

Hopefully, he could draw on that strength right now.

Otto knocked on the door and entered when he heard his father bark out. He entered to see his father sitting at his desk, scribbling away as he worked through the huge ledger. The pen scratched on the paper, making Otto's head ache. He barely glanced up as Otto crossed the room. "May I speak with you, Father?"

"Depends on what you have to say," Darrington grunted. He put his pen down and sat back, taking off his glasses. "Well, what is it? And be quick. I'm busy."

Otto had no intention of being slow. Even then, his father's piercing gaze was unnerving. "I...I wanted to make you a proposition, Father."

"A proposition?"

"Yes. One that would benefit both of us."

Darrington looked sceptical. "I'll be the judge of that." He huffed and waved his hand. "Very well, then. What is this proposition?"

"I don't go to sea. Hear me out, please," he added hurriedly when Darrington started spluttering in protest. "Instead of going to sea, I stay here and work for you. I'll take an apprentice's wage and learn about the business from you. Anything that you're happy with."

Darrington was silent. Otto shuffled from foot to foot. He hated it when his father was quiet in this way. Darrington narrowed his eyes at his son. "So you're determined to be a coward, aren't you?"

Otto's mouth fell open. "I'm not going to war on a merchant ship, Father! And this has nothing to do with being a coward. I just want to be part of your business. I want to learn from you. How can I learn when I'm out at sea?"

"You can learn by seeing how things start at sea."

"But I'm not a sailor, Father. You know that as well as I do." He gestured at the ledger in front of them. "I can do numbers, you know that, and I can read. I prefer the business side of things, anyway. And don't you need someone to carry this on for you in the future?"

Even as he spoke, Darrington was shaking his head. And Otto could feel his heart sinking. "You'll become a sailor," Darrington snapped. "You haven't got a choice."

"Yes, I do," Otto protested. "Why won't you let your only son work for you?"

"Because you're a disgrace." Darrington rose to his feet. His eyes were blazing, his face going red. "I want you to learn how to be useful, Otto. And you can't do that under my feet."

"Father..."

"No. You are not staying in London. I am your father and you will listen to me."

Chapter Nine
No Choice

Otto could feel his anger building. He tried to dampen it, but Darrington's refusal to listen wasn't helping. "I'm a grown man, Father," he pointed out. "I can make my own choices."

Darrington snorted. "Not when you're my son, you don't." He picked up some papers, which he held out to his son. "There's a ship leaving for India in four days. The captain's an old friend of mine. I've already let him know you'll be there. If you don't go, you'll be scorned and treated accordingly." He looked positively gleeful about it. "And I won't have anyone in my family disgrace the rest of us."

Otto could see there was no talking his father out of it. Darrington looked delighted at the thought of getting his son out of his sight. He was ashamed of Otto, and that hit him hard. "I won't go," he growled.

"Oh, you will go. Even if I have to force you on myself." Darrington sat back at his desk, effectively dismissing his son. "Now, get out of my sight. Or I'll have you thrown out."

Otto glared at him, but his father simply ignored him as he picked up his pen, dipped it in the inkwell, and went back to scratching away at the paper. He would just not listen. And Otto knew he would follow through on his threats.

There had to be a way out of it. But as he left the office, Otto didn't know what it would take.

***

Adelle couldn't wait to see Otto. It was her last day working during the day shift before she started the night schedule. Adelle couldn't help but feel excited about the change. She didn't normally like change, but she had high hopes for this one. Hopefully, this would mean more work and more pay. Not many people worked the night shift due to hating the parameters of it, so Adelle was sure there would be a lot for her to do.

It also meant more time to see Otto. She was delighted at the thought. Just being in his company made Adelle feel better. Three months cultivating a courtship with him had certainly turned out better than she anticipated.

It wouldn't be long before Otto was proposing, Adelle was sure of it. She tried to ignore the fact that they weren't of the same social station, and it would be practically out of the question. But Adelle didn't want to think about it. She wanted to think about a life with Otto, starting a family with him. No more poverty for her and Elbert. Adelle knew that love was making her think foolishly, but she didn't care. Being in love felt glorious. She didn't want it to end.

After her shift, Adelle hovered outside the door to the factory. She was beginning to worry. There was no sign of Otto. He was normally there on time if not before Adelle. He had never missed walking her home even if it meant leaving his own shift early.

Where was he?

Adelle began to wonder if something had happened to him. Had Otto been hurt at work? Had he been attacked? Adelle began to panic. What if Otto had been killed?

She was almost in hysterics by the time Otto finally came hurrying into the alley. Adelle burst into tears and ran to him, throwing her arms around him. "Thank God!" she gasped, holding on tight. "I thought something had happened to you."

"Forgive me, Adelle." Otto hugged her tightly. "I had to get out from under my father's watch. He's sure that I'm going to sneak away."

"What do you mean? Sneak away to where?" Then Adelle saw the grave expression on Otto's face. "Otto?"

"He… I…" Otto closed his eyes. "I have to sail in four days. I have no choice about it. If I don't go, I'll be ostracised."

Adelle felt her heart sinking. "What? You…you're going?"

"I'm afraid so." Otto opened his eyes. He looked like he had been backed into a corner. "And I can't do anything about it. I've tried, but Father won't listen. He wouldn't even entertain the idea of me working for him."

"And how long are you going to be away?" Adelle didn't want to know the answer, but she had to. Already, she was starting to feel cold at the idea of Otto leaving.

"A year, at the most."

"A year?" Adelle couldn't breathe. Otto was leaving for a year? Surely this couldn't happen. It couldn't! She pushed away from Otto and hurried out into the street. She couldn't look at him, not when she knew he was going so soon.

"Adelle!" Otto was hurrying after her, catching up to her in the street. "Adelle, please! Wait!" He swung her around, trying to hold her.

But Adelle pushed against him. She could barely see for her tears. "How am I supposed to cope with not seeing you for a year?" she demanded, shoving him in the chest. "You made it sound like things could get better. How can they when you're not here?"

"Adelle..."

"Please, Otto, let me go."

But Otto wouldn't let go. Instead, he tugged her back into the alley, holding her as he moved them into the shadows. Then he kissed her. Adelle stiffened. Otto had kissed her before, but never on the mouth. He had always been a gentleman. This was different. It was...desperate.

She sighed and relaxed into his arms. Her head was telling her to get away, she shouldn't fall any further, but her heart wanted to keep kissing him.

Otto broke the kiss. He sounded breathless, and he hugged Adelle to him. "I'm not letting you go, Adelle. Never," he vowed in a raspy voice. "And I won't leave you."

"You are leaving me, though," Adelle protested. "You're going to India."

"And if I were able to, I'd take you with me." Otto kissed her forehead, cupping her face in his hands. "Look at me, Adelle, please." He wiped her tears off her cheeks with his thumbs. "Do you think I want to leave you? The thought pains me like you can't believe. But you'll still have my heart. That won't leave you."

"What...what are you saying, Otto?"

"I'm saying that I love you, Adelle. Ever since we met. You know I'm not the soppiest of people, but when it comes to you, I cannot help it." He kissed her again. "I love you."

"I..." Adelle's head was spinning. Otto had said the words she had longed to hear, and now it felt surreal. "I don't know what to say."

"Don't say anything. Just hear me out." Otto rested his forehead against hers before kissing her again. "I was going to ask you to marry me on your birthday. Make you my wife. That's all I want to do."

"Otto..."

"I have to go to sea. I have no choice." Otto ran his hands through her hair, her pins clattering to the ground. Then he gathered her back in his arms. "But I'll make sure you get the money I send back to England. I'll make sure you're looked after, that you can have a roof over your head and food in your belly. I'll look after you from afar. Then when I come back, we'll be married."

"You..." Adelle stared up at him. "You want to marry me?"

"You're still stuck on that part?"

"No one's asked me to marry them before." Adelle rested her cheek against his chest. "I didn't think it would ever happen."

"Well, it's happened." Otto stroked her hair, cradling her against his chest. "It's going to take time, but I'm willing to wait if you are."

Adelle didn't need to think about it. She already knew her answer. She was nodding before Otto had finished speaking. "Yes, I can wait. Even if you end up being incredibly soppy."

Otto chuckled. "Don't expect it very often."

"I won't hold my breath." Adelle stroked his cheek. "Just don't leave me until the last minute."

"I won't."

***

Otto was in a better mood as he headed back home. Adelle had accepted his proposal. He couldn't have topped the mood he was in right now. The knowledge he was going to sea felt like less of an evil now. It would be long and arduous, a journey that Otto was not looking forward to. But it paid well, and he would be able to send a sizeable amount of his wages back to Adelle. She would be able to look after herself and Elbert with what Otto earned.

Only a year. It wasn't going to be an easy year, but it was just one year. Then Otto would be able to marry Adelle. They could start over, and Otto could start up his own business. Anything he could think of. They wouldn't struggle at all. And Adelle wouldn't have to work herself into the grave as she tried to figure out where the next pennies were coming from. She wouldn't be starving or ill because she was focused on her brother.

Otto wanted to take care of her. That's all he wanted to do.

He was whistling as he entered his home. Adelle started the night shift the next day, so wouldn't be going in until the evening. Otto would be able to sneak away to walk her in, and then he would be there in the morning when she went home. Anything to keep seeing her until the last possible moment.

But Otto's good mood dissipated when he saw his mother hurry into the hall. She looked decidedly nervous. Then Otto could hear his father pacing around with heavy footsteps in the front room, muttering to himself.

"Otto!" Sarah hurried to her son's side. "Where have you been? Your father is in a rage."

"He's always in a rage."

"Not like this. He keeps saying something about you and a girl?"

Otto froze. He didn't need to guess who his father was talking about. While they hadn't kept it a secret, Otto had made sure nobody who knew his father had seen him. Evidently it hadn't worked.

"Adelle," he murmured.

Sarah's eyes widened. "It's true? She's the one you've been sneaking out to see all the time?"

"She's the girl who sewed up my clothes last year." Otto swallowed. "I love her, Mother. And she loves me." He could say that to his mother without consequence. Sarah was an open-minded woman with a soft heart. Otto could commit murder, and she would happily help him bury the body.

Unfortunately, from his reaction, his father didn't share the same sentiment.

Sarah nudged him towards the front room. "You'd better talk to him, Otto."

"Talk to him? I'll be lucky if I can get a word in." Otto sighed and patted Sarah's arm. "Don't worry, Mother, I'll go in."

Everything in Otto wanted to run the other way. But that wasn't going to stop the tirade. His mother didn't need to see this. Otto entered the front room in time to see his father pick up a small vase and throw it across the room. Otto dodged out of the way, watching it smash into the wall where his head had been.

"What the... Father!"

Darrington was snarling. Otto had seen him angry before, but never like this. His father advanced on him. "How could you?"

"What?"

"How could you get into a relationship with a chit like that girl on the docks?"

Otto snorted. "You make it sound sordid, Father. We've never done anything wrong."

"You haven't done anything wrong?" Darrington bellowed. "My source tells me that girl is a seamstress. A lowly one, at that. One you shouldn't even be breathing the same air with. From what I've been told, you two have been walking out together for a while. And looking like complete fools."

Otto growled. He wasn't backing down this time. Not when Adelle was involved.

Chapter Ten
A New Start

"Adelle is not lowly, Father. She's a good person. I love her."

"You love her?" Darrington snorted rudely. "You don't know anything about love. You're just a boy."

"I'm three-and-twenty. I more than know about it."

"From those ridiculous Walter Scott novels that your mother leaves lying about? There is no such thing as love. That doesn't get anyone anywhere."

"You married Mother," Otto pointed out. "You must have loved her."

But Darrington only rolled his eyes and kicked at his armchair. "It's called a marriage of convenience, boy. She was the daughter of someone I needed important contacts from. There is some affection for her, I'll admit, but that's it. I don't love your mother."

Otto was horrified. He had never heard anything like that. How could anyone not love his mother? And to be spoken about so coldly… "Does Mother know?"

"Oh, she knows. Even since the start." His father was so blasé about it. "Like I said, love doesn't exist. That's just for fantasists and pathetic writers of romance novels."

"I'm not a fantasist, Father," Otto snapped. "And Adelle is worth it. You should meet her..."

"I don't want to meet her!" Darrington bellowed. "I don't want you to see her again!"

Otto barked out a laugh. He wasn't a little boy. He was a grown man. His father couldn't stop him from making up his mind now. "You haven't got a choice on that, Father. We'll be getting married when I get back."

Now Darrington looked like he was about to explode. His face was bright red, his eyes were bulging, and he looked close to frothing at the mouth.

Otto was surprised he didn't drop down dead at that point.

"No!" Darrington snarled. "You won't be marrying her."

"I don't need your permission, Father."

"Yes, you do." Darrington advanced on him, jabbing a finger into Otto's face. "I'll make sure you never see her again, if it's the last thing I do. You will be getting on that ship, and I'll make sure you stay in India permanently. You won't see England again."

"You can't force me!"

"Yes, I can." Darrington grabbed Otto by the scruff of his neck and shoved him towards the door. "Get out of here. You're going to your room, and you're not leaving until I say so."

Otto shook him off, squaring up to his father. "How can you stop me from leaving?" he demanded.

That was when his father punched him in the face.

***

The fight hadn't lasted long. Almost as soon as Otto started grappling, his mother and their footman Bailey had come in to separate them. Darrington had been spluttering and raging, pushing all sorts of threats on his son. Otto had been hauled out by his mother, who cleaned him up and urged him upstairs. There wasn't anything he could do now.

Otto would have to wait until the morning to talk to his father again; if he would agree to talk. He had to get out of this somehow. Otto was not going to live in India permanently. That was out of the question. As he went to bed, Otto kept playing over and over in his mind what he was going to say to his father. But every scenario ended in an argument. Otto just couldn't find the right thing to say, even in his own mind.

It prevented him from sleeping that night until shortly before dawn. Otto just couldn't put his mind to ease. Whenever he wasn't thinking about what to say to his father, he was thinking about Adelle. He couldn't stay in India. Not now, not unless he had Adelle.

Just before he fell off to sleep, Otto made up his mind. If his father refused to let him stay, Otto would find a way to bring Adelle and Elbert with him. He would look after them wherever they were.

Otto wasn't sure how long he had slept, but he was startled awake by a loud scream. He rubbed the sleep from his eyes and sat up, his ears ringing with another scream. Scrambling out of bed, Otto grabbed for his robe and shrugged it on as he headed into the hallway. His mother came out from her bedroom across the hall, tying the belt of her own robe.

"Mother? What's happened?"

"I don't know. That wasn't me screaming."

Then the scream started again. It was coming from his father's room at the far end of the hall. Otto was there as their maid Harriet stumbled out of the bedroom. Her face was pasty white, and she was crying.

Otto grabbed her before she sagged to the floor. "Harriet! What's the matter?"

"It...It's Mr Darrington." Harriet gasped. She started to cry. "He's...he..."

Otto could feel his blood going cold. Shifting Harriet over to Sarah, Otto entered his father's bedroom. And the sight before him made him fall to his knees.

***

Adelle was still sleeping in preparation for her night shift when someone came knocking. She answered it to see a young man dressed in smart clothes, who wordlessly shoved a note into her hand. It was from Otto, asking her to come at once.

Adelle was confused. What did that mean? What was Otto up to? Adelle could only hope it wasn't to meet his father; from the stories Otto had told her about him, she didn't want to be anywhere near him.

But Adelle wasn't about to argue. Especially when the young messenger was looking shifty. She dressed hurriedly and followed him back to Otto's higher class neighbourhood. These were better houses for those with money; the supervisors and the businessmen lived here.

It was just seeing his house for the first time that made Adelle realise that they were completely different. How they had fallen in love when their circumstances were vastly opposite, Adelle had no idea. But it had happened.

The footman ushered her inside, and Adelle found herself in a hallway that seemed to be bigger than the rooms she lived in. A handsome woman in her forties was coming down the stairs, dressed in black. Adelle froze. That was a mourning dress. What had happened to Otto? Adelle began to panic.

The woman got to the bottom of the stairs and approached Adelle with a gentle smile. "Oh, my dear, don't look so scared. Otto's quite alive. Calm yourself."

"I..." Adelle allowed the woman to take her hands. They were warm even with no gloves on. "Forgive me, I...I didn't know what to think."

"You thought my son was dead, didn't you?"

Adelle nodded wordlessly. This had to be Otto's mother. She certainly had her son's complexion and colourings. She seemed too sweet, even with pain and sadness in her eyes.

"That, I'm afraid, goes to my husband. He...he had a heart attack during the night and died in his sleep. Gave my maid quite a scare when she brought him his breakfast."

"Oh." Adelle's mind went blank. She swallowed. "I...I'm so sorry for your loss, Mrs Darrington."

"Thank you, my dear." Mrs Darrington smiled and nodded towards a closed door. "My son is in there. He's very eager to speak to you."

"How is he?"

"He's coping. He saw his father dead, and it shook him a little." Mrs Darrington patted her hand and urged her towards the door. "I think seeing you will make him feel better."

Adelle didn't need to be told twice. Barely pausing to knock, she entered the front room. Otto was standing by the window, staring out into the street. He was dressed in black, looking very solemn. Adelle closed the door and approached him. Seeing him in this state made things different. It was like she had never seen him before.

Suddenly, she felt nervous around him. "Otto?"

Otto turned. His eyes lit up when he saw her. "Adelle."

Then he was approaching, holding out his arms. Adelle didn't need asking twice. She ran to him, allowing Otto to sweep her off her feet and spin her around. He settled her back on her feet and stroked her hair from her face.

"Forgive me for calling for you so early. I know you were trying to rest for tonight."

"It's absolutely fine. I would come no matter the time." Adelle cupped his jaw. "I'm so sorry about your father. I know he wasn't a kind man, but no one deserves to go through that."

"Thank you." Otto kissed her palm. "You've always had such a sweet heart, even for the harshest of people. That's what I love about you."

Adelle bit her lip. "What does this mean for you?"

"You mean me going to sea?"

"Yes. I know we shouldn't be talking about it now," Adelle added hurriedly, "but under the circumstances..."

"No, I'm not going." Otto smiled. "I'm staying here."

Adelle couldn't believe her ears. She hugged him tightly, feeling Otto's arms tighten around her. "Thank God."

"There are some things I have to do, however." Otto sighed, easing Adelle back. "It's Society's customs, and I have to follow them."

"What sort of things?"

"I have to take over the business my father left behind, and I have to look after my mother." Otto hesitated. "I also have to go into mourning. Which means I can't associate in Society with others, and I cannot marry. Not yet."

He could not marry. Adelle knew about mourning. She had wanted to follow it herself, but circumstances had stopped that. Otto would have to retire from Society while he mourned his father. She took a deep breath. "How long do you have to be in mourning for? And where does that leave us?"

"A year, at the most. If I'm lucky, only six months." Otto kissed her forehead. "But it doesn't change what there is between us. I won't stop seeing you, and I certainly won't stop loving you."

That had Adelle sagging against him. "Thank God. You had me frightened for a moment."

"You thought I was going to reject you because of my circumstances?"

"A little."

Otto laughed. He gathered her against his side and urged her over to an armchair. Making her sit, he knelt before her and took her hands. He was still smiling. "Adelle, I'm not going to turn my back on you because I have to mourn my father's passing. I am in charge of a bigger fortune now. I will be able to look after you and run this household, and things will be fine. You and Elbert will not go without."

"I don't want to impose on you, Otto."

"We've been through this before. You are not imposing on me."

"But people will talk!"

Otto snorted. "And I'd rather look after you than have you put into the workhouse. As soon as my mourning period is over, we can be married. And we won't have to hide anything." He raised his eyebrows. "That is, if you still want to marry me?"

Adelle couldn't stop herself. She giggled, throwing her arms around Otto's neck as she kissed him. "Of course I still want to marry you, you fool." She laughed. "I wouldn't want anything less."

Otto let out a shuddering sigh and hugged her tightly. "Thank God for that."

Epilogue:

18 months later:

"They're sweet, aren't they?"

Adelle laughed. She and her mother-in-law were sitting on the terrace watching as Otto and Elbert played badminton in the garden. Elbert had only started playing it a few days before, and now he was making Otto run around chasing the shuttlecock.

"I wouldn't call Elbert sweet. That's the last thing you could call him."

Sarah smiled. "Well, I would call him sweet. He's a kind boy."

"And practically a man. He's just turned sixteen now."

Sixteen years old, and Elbert was rapidly changing physically. He was broader and stronger than before, taking on work at Otto's business. Otto had taken Elbert on as an apprentice, and the past year had built a strong bond between them. Otto treated Elbert like his own brother, which Adelle loved.

They had brought Elbert to live with them in Otto's home shortly after Otto and Adelle finally married following Valentine's Day. His mother also lived with them, which Adelle was happy with. Now that she had the chance to associate with the woman, she found the older Mrs

Darrington to be a kind, generous lady. It was no wonder that Otto had inherited that side from her.

Adelle could hardly believe it. A year ago, she had been close to losing Otto at sea. Now she was married, not needing to work as hard as she once had, if at all, and Adelle found she was happy. Relaxed and happy.

That was a state she had never expected to be in.

Sarah put her teacup and saucer aside, setting it on the tray between them. She was still wearing her mourning dress, but she was looking more alive and vibrant than before. "How are you feeling today, dear?"

"A little better." Adelle pressed a hand to her belly. "My stomach is still churning, but I haven't been sick yet."

"That's good. I was beginning to get worried." Sarah paused. "You might want Doctor Farnsworth to take a look at you, Adelle."

"Why? There's the influenza going around at the moment. I wouldn't be surprised if it's the start of that."

But Sarah was shaking her head, still smiling. "I don't think so. When I was expecting Otto, I was exactly like you."

It took a moment for the penny to drop. Adelle stared at her mother-in-law. "You mean...I could be carrying a child?"

"I think so. You're showing all the signs. You need that new chapter in your life, Adelle." Sarah patted her daughter-in-law's hand. "This would be perfect for you."

A baby. Adelle had always thought about having children. But she was never in the right position to have one. No money and no husband. Now she had both. It felt like a miracle.

She looked over at Otto, who was laughing along with Elbert as they knocked the shuttlecock back and forth. "Do you think Otto will be pleased?"

"He'll be delighted. He's always wanted children. My husband…" Sarah sighed. "He only wanted one boy to carry on the business. And Otto missed having a brother or sister." She nodded at her son. "Why don't you go and tell him? That really will make his day."

"In a moment." Adelle sipped at her tea, smiling at the older woman. "I want to bask in the knowledge that I'm about to become a mother a little while longer."

Sarah laughed. "I don't blame you, love. I don't blame you."

*** The End ***

If you enjoyed this story, could I please ask you to leave a review on Amazon.

Printed in Great Britain
by Amazon